PUBLIC LIBRARY
DISTRICT OF COLUMBIA

Six
Silly Foxes

Six
Silly Foxes

Alex Moran
Illustrated by Keith Baker

Green Light Readers
Harcourt, Inc.
Orlando   Austin   New York   San Diego   London

We are six silly foxes—
Ellen, Max, and Greg.

We are six silly foxes—
Dixon, Beth, and Meg.

How can six silly foxes hop

on boxes filled with eggs?

We are six sad foxes. Look at that! Oh no!
We are six sad foxes, very sad. It is so.

How can six sad foxes fix an old banjo?

We are six hungry foxes, and it's time
to eat. We are six hungry foxes
looking for a sweet.

How can six hungry foxes snack
on ice cream in the heat?

We are six mad foxes, as mad as mad
can be. We are six mad foxes.
(Add it up—three and three.)

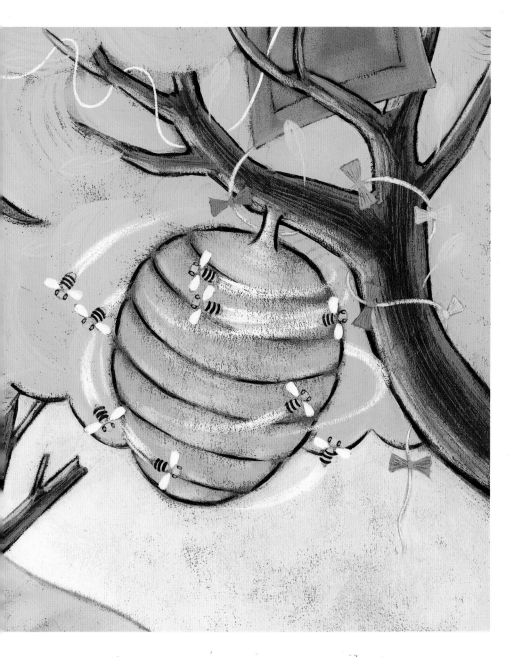

How can six mad foxes jump
into the next tree?

We are six happy foxes,
very happy, you can see.

We are six happy foxes.
You ask how that can be?

Silly or sad, hungry or mad,

we are all so very happy
in this mixed-up family!

Places to Play

The six silly foxes in this story played everywhere.
What do you like to do when you're inside and outside?

WHAT YOU'LL NEED

paper

crayons or markers

1 Fold a piece of paper in half. Write INSIDE and OUTSIDE at the top.

2 Make a list of all the games and activities you like to do inside and outside.

INSIDE
· play house
· read books
· do puzzles
· play school
· build with
   blocks

OUTSIDE
· jump rope
· ride bikes
· play soccer
· play tag
· play on the
   playground

3 Fold another piece of paper in half. Write INSIDE and OUTSIDE at the top.

4 Draw a picture and write a sentence about each of your favorite things to do inside and outside.

INSIDE
I like to read before bed.

OUTSIDE
I play catch with Sparky outside.

Share your ideas with a friend.

Then go and play—
inside and outside!

Meet the Illustrator

Keith Baker was a teacher before he went to art school. He writes and illustrates stories that he knows children in his classes would have enjoyed. He says teaching was fun, but he really loves creating books.

He hopes you enjoy reading them!

© 1998 Joseph Rupp/Black Star

Keith Baker

Copyright © 2000 by Harcourt, Inc.

All rights reserved. No part of this publication may be reproduced or transmitted in any form or by any means, electronic or mechanical, including photocopy, recording, or any information storage and retrieval system, without permission in writing from the publisher.

For information about permission to reproduce selections from this book, please write to Permissions, Houghton Mifflin Harcourt Publishing Company 215 Park Avenue South NY, NY 10003.

www.hmhco.com

First Green Light Readers edition 2000
Green Light Readers is a trademark of Harcourt, Inc., registered in the United States of America and/or other jurisdictions.

The Library of Congress has cataloged an earlier edition as follows:
Moran, Alex.
Six silly foxes/Alex Moran; illustrated by Keith Baker.
p.   cm.
"Green Light Readers."
Summary: A family of foxes experiences a wide range of emotions and needs over the course of a day.
[1. Foxes—Fiction.   2. Family life—Fiction.]
I. Baker, Keith, 1953– ill.   II. Title.
PZ7.M788193Si   2000
[E]—dc21   99-6813
ISBN 978-0-15-204823-5
ISBN 978-0-15-204863-1 (pb)

SCP   10 9
4500514102

Ages 4-6
Grade: 1-2
Guided Reading Level: G-H
Reading Recovery Level: 14-15

Green Light Readers
For the reader who's ready to GO!

"A must-have for any family with a beginning reader."—*Boston Sunday Herald*

"You can't go wrong with adding several copies of these terrific books to your beginning-to-read collection."—*School Library Journal*

"A winner for the beginner."—*Booklist*

Five Tips to Help Your Child Become a Great Reader

1. Get involved. Reading aloud to and with your child is just as important as encouraging your child to read independently.

2. Be curious. Ask questions about what your child is reading.

3. Make reading fun. Allow your child to pick books on subjects that interest her or him.

4. Words are everywhere—not just in books. Practice reading signs, packages, and cereal boxes with your child.

5. Set a good example. Make sure your child sees YOU reading.

Why Green Light Readers Is the Best Series for Your New Reader

● Created exclusively for beginning readers by some of the biggest and brightest names in children's books

● Reinforces the reading skills your child is learning in school

● Encourages children to read—and finish—books by themselves

● Offers extra enrichment through fun, age-appropriate activities unique to each story

● Incorporates characteristics of the Reading Recovery program used by educators

● Developed with Harcourt School Publishers and credentialed educational consultants